D0903436

DISCARD

PLÁTANOS
Go with Everything

Written by Lissette Norman

Illustrated by Sara Palacios

HARPER
An Imprint of HarperCollinsPublishers

Plátanos are like golden slices of this afternoon's sun on our dinner plates.

I help Mami cook in the kitchen.

She shares stories about life in the Dominican Republic before my older brother, Kendry, and I were born.

Mami's stories are the secret ingredient in all her yummy food.

When the chicken, beans, and rice are nearly cooked, Mami peels the plátanos with a knife.

First she cuts off both ends. Then Mami slides the blade down the plátano.

As her fingers separate the thick green skin from the pale-yellow flesh inside, I ask, "Why do Dominicans love plátanos so much?"
Mami smiles and answers, "Because they remind us of home, Yesenia."

"Back home, plátanos grow upward on trees," Mami says, and I wonder how that's even possible.

"Plátanos are long and heavy, so they droop and curve as they grow, but their feet are always reaching for the stars."

That is so cool, I think.

Plátanos are like warm hello kisses from Abuela, who arrives early for dinner with Abuelo. They both lived with us in our apartment when they first came to the United States.

Six of us in an apartment meant for four took some getting used to after living in a big house in the Dominican Republic. Even though it's great to have my room back, I miss them. And I'm glad their new place is still close to ours.

Plátanos are like a love letter
from the Dominican Republic.

My parents moved to New York City to make a better life for
me and my brother. But a long string of plátanos keeps them
tied to their homeland as if they're two flapping kites.

Sweet slices of maduros frying in the pan remind me of Mami's dream of owning a house with a garden. Crispy, salt-sprinkled tostones are like symbols of Papi's hope for a quiet office to write his poetry.

The smell of their wishes is
everywhere in our apartment.
It slides out of our window
and floats on and on.

BAGELS SMITH
168 st.
NEWS
STORE 99¢
168 Street Station
A C 1
Eddie's
SINCE 1946
ICE COLD BEVERAGES
HOT DOGS
LEMONADE
SUBWAY

Plátanos are like baskets of green treasure we find
inside our corner bodega.
My three tías, two tíos, and five bouncy cousins stop
by for a visit.
So Mami asks Papi to go buy more plátanos for dinner,
and I tag along.

Papi says when people visit our home and we serve them a plate of sunny-side up eggs, fried Dominican salami and cheese with mashed plátanos, what we're really saying is "Welcome! So glad you're here!"

When Dominicans offer you tender, love-filled mangú, it means "You're family now!"

Plátanos are like the love poems Papi recites to Mami from outside our building. Mami listens from our second-floor window, all rosy-cheeked and smiling.

Plátanos are like a magical cure.
I studied hard all week for my classroom spelling bee
this morning.
But I missed the first *H* in *RHYTHM* and lost.

When I got home from school, Mami cheered me up,
promising to make my favorite dessert after dinner: caramelized
plátanos with a scoop of ice cream and sprinkled cinnamon.
She reminded me that plátanos can heal a broken heart.

Plátanos are like superpowers.

Kendry *swears* plátano magic is behind every pitch and home run by the Dominican baseball players Pedro Martínez, Robinson Canó, and Juan Soto.

Plátanos are like a fiesta. This Friday, as always, there is so much laughter, music, and dancing. My tíos clear the coffee table out of the living room. Mami blasts her favorite merengue song.

We sing at the tops of our voices "Kulikitaka ti. Kulikitaka ta." Music fills the spaces our laughter can't reach. Everybody shakes their hips from side to side. My worries are all put away as Papi spins me round and round.

The smell of Mami's delicious food drifts into the living room. Mami gives me sweet bites of plátanos and I sway to the music as the flavors dance on my tongue.